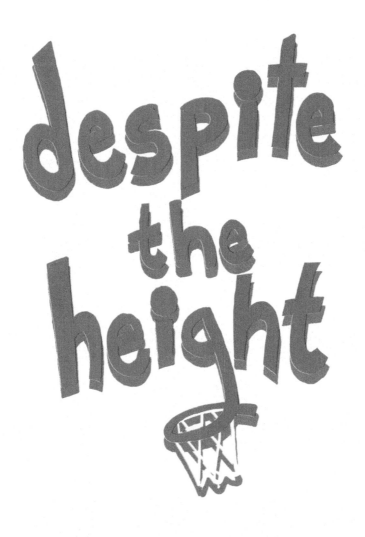

despite the height

By Ivory Latta
and Charles R. Smith, Jr.

Illustrated by D.J. Coffman

Editor: Amy Ashby

ISBN: 978-1-943258-41-3 (hard cover)
        978-1-943258-42-0 (soft cover)
Library of Congress: 2017942544

Published by Warren Publishing
Charlotte, NC
www.warrenpublishing.net
Printed in the United States

I would like to dedicate this book to my parents, brothers, and sisters.
Thank you all for your unwavering support. My dream has
come true and it has been amazing to share this journey with my family.

I value all of you! I pray for your continued
good health, happiness, and prosperity.

Thanks and love to you!

—Ivory

BOUNCE. BOUNCE. BOUNCE-BOUNCE. BOUNCE B-BOUNCE. BOUNCE BOUNCE.

Life in the Latta household was not quiet. Not with the youngest, Ivory, bouncing her basketball off the walls at the crack of dawn.

BOUNCE. BOUNCE.

BOUNCE BOUNCE.

BOUNCE BOUNCE BOUNCE.

BOUNCE. BOUNCE.

B-BOUNCE!

Off the floor. Off the wall. Off the door.

BOUNCE BOUNCE.

"Let's go play some ball!"

Five simple words brought all seven Latta kids and their dad together every day on the worn, dirt court.

Ivory was small, but her brothers were not. They pushed her around and roughed her up. Still, despite her height, Ivory didn't quit or back down.

"You ain't pushing me around," Ivory would say before darting past her big brothers' reaching hands.

But it wasn't enough.
Her big brothers won every single time.

BOUNCE BOUNCE. BOUNCE BOUNCE. B-BOUNCE BOUNCE!

"Got you, Ivory! Where you at?" Dad said on his way to an easy layup.

"Aw, mannnnn. You got me again, Dad. How'd you get so good?"

"Simple," Dad said. "Practice like you play."

So she tried harder. From sunup to sundown, Ivory dribbled like it was her job. BOUNCE after BOUNCE. Hour after hour. Day after day.

Dribble with the left hand. Dribble with the right hand. Dribble left to right. Dribble right to left. Dribble fast. Dribble slow. Dribble high. Dribble low.

Dribble off the walls. Dribble off the floor.
Dribble through the hall. Dribble off the door.
Ivory dribbled and dribbled and dribbled her
ball until it became a part of her hand.

Despite her height, she would not lose to
her brothers anymore.

As Dad played, Ivory played, too.
Her moves mirrored his on offense.
Dribble left. Dribble right. Cross right to left.
Left to right. Off to the hoop.

Dribble-dribble forward. Dribble back slow.
Dribble-dribble forward. Off to the hoop.
Ivory faked Dad out more than a few times,
but Dad got past her defense.

"Come on Ivory, hustle. Put some pep in your step," Dad said. "Move your feet on defense. If you want to be good, you have to play both sides of the floor."

So Ivory shuffled—slowly at first.
Shuffle. Shuffle. Shuffle.
Dad BOUNCE-BOUNCED left to right, then zipped past Ivory to the basket. Again. And again.
But Ivory wouldn't quit.

Ivory shuffled faster. And faster. And faster. And soon the BOUNCE-BOUNCE became BOUNCE BOUNCE BOUNCE B-BOUNCE BOUNCE B-BOUNCE BOUNCE BOUNCE as Dad worked to shake Ivory.

"I locked you up, Dad!" Ivory said.
"Yes you did," Dad said. "But I still got a few tricks up my sleeve!"
"Alright, Dad. Show me what you got!"

Dad BOUNCE-BOUNCED-BOUNCED hard to his right, but Ivory matched him step for step. He hit the breaks and launched a soft jump shot to the rim. SWISH. Nothing but net.

"Awww, man!" Ivory shouted. "How'd you do that, Dad? Teach me that jump shot." "Now, if I teach you that," Dad said, "it's all over."

They laughed. Then played.
BOUNCE after BOUNCE. Shot after shot.
Point after point. Game after game. Ivory
missed more jump shots than she made.
"Just square up your shoulders to the
basket and they'll start falling," Dad said.

Ivory began putting all the pieces of her game together. Bounce right. Cross left. BOUNCE-BOUNCE-BOUNCE. Off to the hoop for a layup.

Ivory was still small, and her brothers were still much bigger. But that didn't keep her from challenging one of her brothers to yet another game of one-on-one.

"I'm ready for you, Suron," Ivory boasted. "You talk a big game, little girl," he said, before tossing her the ball.

Ivory BOUNCE-BOUNCE-BOUNCED her way
to the basket on offense, and shuffle-shuffle-
shuffled her feet to keep up on defense.

Soon, Ivory was just one point away from her
first win over her big brother.

"Alright, Ivory," he said. "I get it, you can
dribble and get to the hoop. Let's see what
else you got. Betchu can't win on a jump shot.
I'll even give it to you."

"No no no," Ivory protested. "I don't want
no gimmes. Play me straight up."

Ivory stood her forty-four-inch frame at the top of the key, the ball rested on her hip.

Suron stood one foot in front of his little sister, left hand down near the ball, right hand up near Ivory's face.

Ivory BOUNCE-BOUNCED with her right hand—slowly.

Suron stayed in front of Ivory, waving his hands to distract her. A quick BOUNCE-BOUNCE to the right, and Ivory took off toward the basket.

Suron backpedaled to stay with her, but this time, Ivory hit the brakes. Suron stumbled backward.

Ivory squared up her shoulders, just like Dad taught her, and floated a rainbow to the rim.

The Real Ivory Latta

I was born September 25, 1984, to Charles and Chenna Latta. I entered the world vivaciously and eager to meet my six older siblings. Upon delivery, it was not indicated that I suffered from asthma, so everything seemed perfect. At three weeks, my parents were thrown for a loop when I suffered my first asthma attack. My breathing was staggered and I struggled to breathe. My parents rushed me to the hospital where I was administered medication, breathing treatments, and sedation. It was very hard on our family.

Following the first asthma attack, I was hospitalized consistently over the next thirteen months off and on. My parents would take me to the hospital and I would stay at least one week a month. Even though my temperature would rise during an asthma attack, I would always have a smile on my face. The frequent hospital visits became my normal.

Even though my asthma took up a lot of time, my parents had to work. Other family members were hesitant to watch me due to my intense asthma attacks. My Aunt Willie Mae was the only person in my family who wasn't afraid of my asthma. She provided me with unconditional love and comfort throughout my entire life.

During one attack when I was four years old, my mom started crying; she was desperate and just wanted me better. I looked at her and said, "I don't have asthma anymore. Don't cry." After that, my mom said my asthma got better.

When I was four, my dad played baseball. I loved to run the bases and pretend I was a baseball player, despite my asthma. I had asthma, but I didn't let it control me; I was rambunctious and I loved sports.

I took an interest in basketball at an early age. My brothers and dad played and I loved watching it on TV. During that time, we had a dirt court. Kids across the neighborhood would come out and play. I loved it, especially competing against the boys.

Around age 10, I started playing in the Amateur Athletic Union (AAU) with the Carolina Stompers, where my dad was a coach. The practices and games were intense, but I loved traveling and meeting new people. The Carolina Stompers won a lot of championships and many of my teammates went on to play at the college level. I also won an AAU championship with Team North Carolina alongside Camille Little.

In the 7th Grade, I played on the York Junior High School team. During my first game, I scored 43 points and was immediately moved to varsity with my two older sisters.

I played varsity basketball at York Comprehension High for the remainder of my high school career. Arsonia Stroud was my coach and was instrumental in setting the foundation for my future in basketball. While I played for York Comprehensive High's Cougars, our team won a championship. I also became the top scorer for men's and women's basketball in South Carolina, Despite being only 5'6".

During my time at UNC Chapel Hill, I received the following accolades:
- ACC Rookie of the Year,
- the Nancy Lieberman Award,
- ACC Player of the Year,
- 2006 Player of the Year by ESPN.com

...And many more.

Points averaged per game:
- 14.0 as a freshman
- 16.2 as a senior
- 16.6 career high

After high school, I participated in the 2003 WBCA High School All-America Game where I scored seventeen points, and earned MVP honors. I then attended UNC Chapel Hill and was coached by the legendary Sylvia Hatchell.

In 2007, I was drafted for the WNBA to the Detroit Shock, becoming one of the smallest women to play professional ball. Since then I've played with other WNBA teams: Atlanta Dream, Tulsa Shock, and currently the Washington Mystics. While playing in the WNBA, I've been to the WNBA All Star Game and have participated in community service projects to help make a difference.

As a kid, I never dreamed I'd play professional basketball, but now I get to do what I love for a living. In short (no pun intended), I've learned to never give up!

"Never give up!"

What are your dreams and goals? Write them down here.

CPSIA information can be obtained
at www.ICGtesting.com
Printed in the USA
BVOW05*0203080617

486134BV00002B/4/P